This is Ebba...

WRITTEN AND ILLUSTRATED BY
SARAH A. SCHROEDER
AND CHRISTOPHER SCHROEDER

For Mara Jean & Luca Roy

First Edition: May 2021
ISBN 978-1-09837-170-8

Hebrews 10:24

This is Ebba.

Ebba started life off the way all sea turtles do.

As an egg.

Most sea turtle nests have over 100 eggs,
but for an unknown reason
Ebba was the only one in hers.

One morning, under the hot summer sun, Ebba started to crack.

PECK-POKE-PROD-PUSH

and finally...

Ebba pushed her way through her delicate barrier and out into the open air.

Ebba felt the cool mist.
She smelt the salty air
and then she felt the sun.

The hot sun.

Quickly instict kicked in
and Ebba started to slowly (*quite slowly*)
drag her small body towards
the sound of crashing waves.

Ebba didn't know how long
it would take to get to the ocean,
or even why she had to get there,
but she kept going feeling it urgent.

But finally after all the struggle
Ebba started to feel the dry sand
turn cool and damp under her body.
She was there!
All she had to do now...

...was dive in.

CRASH PUSH tumble WHIP!

Ebba was aggressively tossed around,
unable to tell which way was up or which way was down.
Then, as suddenly as it had begun...

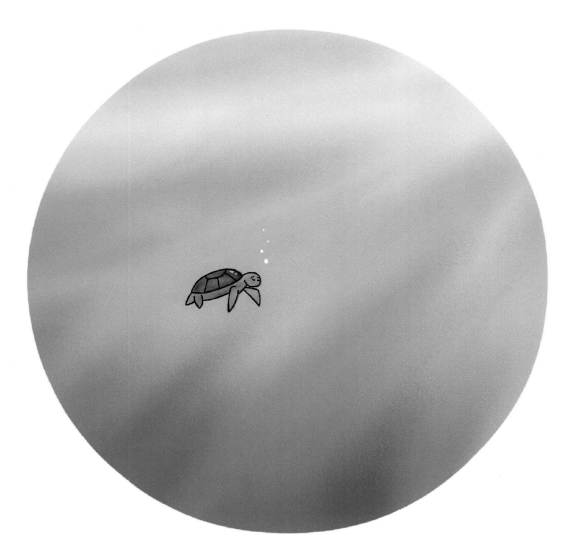

...it was still.

It was DEEP.

It was *silent*.

It was **e m p t y**.

Ebba let the current move her forward.

While heading nowhere in particular
she started to notice the things around her.

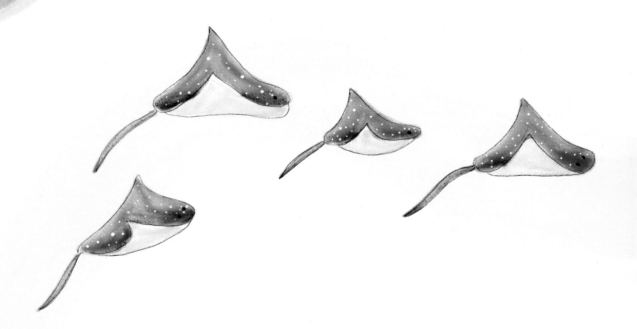

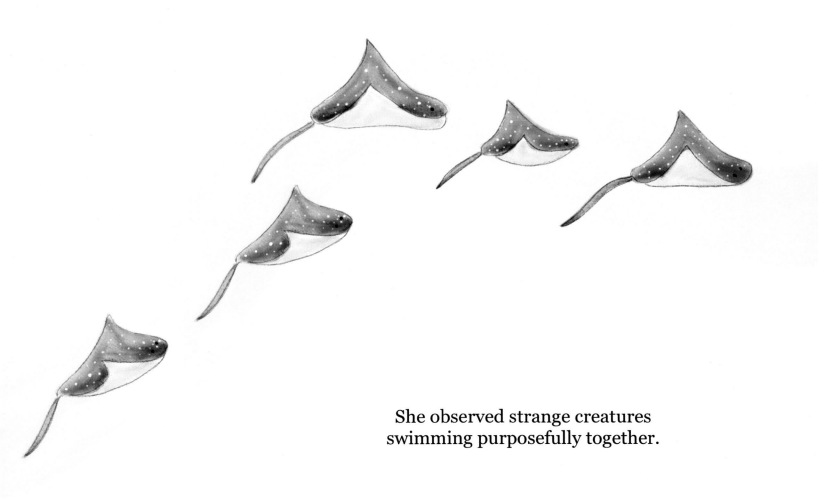

She observed strange creatures
swimming purposefully together.

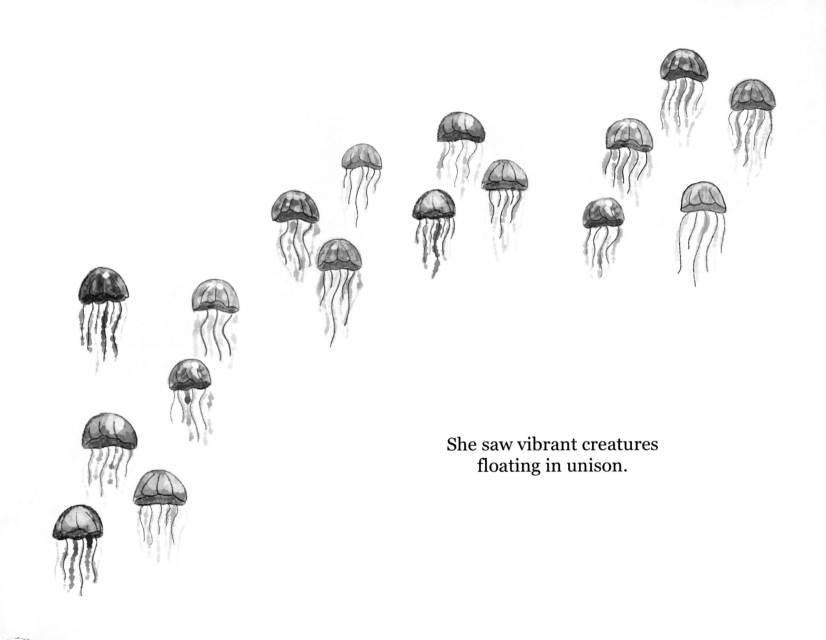

She saw vibrant creatures
floating in unison.

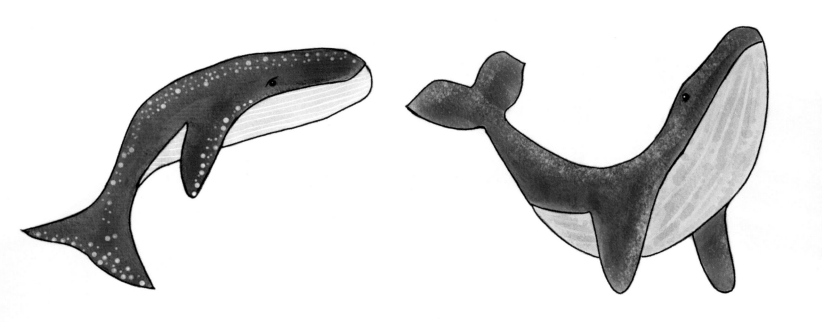

She spotted magnificent creatures
majestically moving as one.

Feeling quite alone as well as quite tired
Ebba's heart started to weigh heavy,
sinking her...

lower...

and lower...

and lower...

...until she was nestled into the comfort of the ocean floor.

This is Irving.

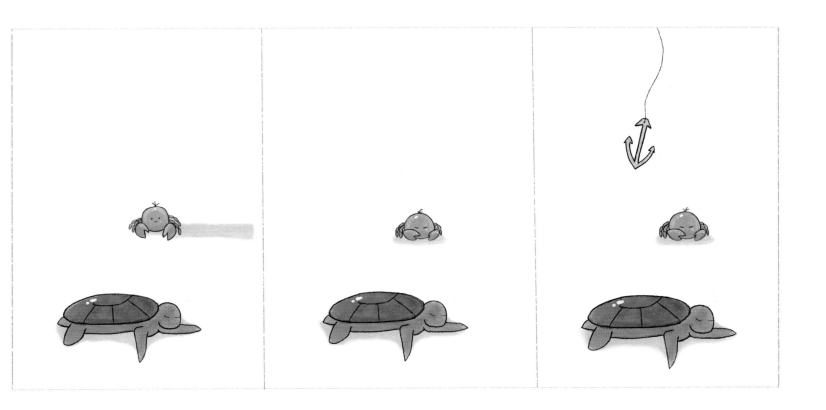

The small, coral colored crab was shuffling along the ocean floor,
heading nowhere in particular, when he came across a dozing sea turtle, Ebba.
After noticing how deeply asleep she was he decided that he, too, deserved a rest.

cr-**THUNK**-ck

Out of nowhere a boat's anchor cut through the water
and landed tragically in the middle of Ebba's back!

thunk...   crack...   creek...

What could she do?!

Ebba was starting to lose hope
as well as her breath.

Irving then awoke in shock
to see his napping partner in distress.

He quickly scurried next to Ebba,
politely introduced himself,
and began to work on getting her free.

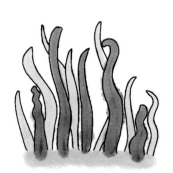

He **HEAVED** and he **HOED**

and he *PUSHED* and he PULLED

and he *grunted* and he *grumbled*

and he YANKED and he **lifted**

and...

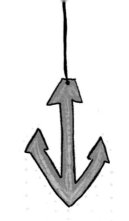

. . . "You're free!"

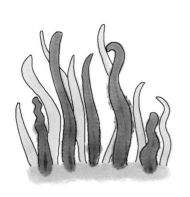

Although it had been difficult to breathe under the weight of the anchor,
Irving's humble attention made her heart feel light.

Ebba had no idea how to react
so she simply smiled and thanked him.
He told her it was his pleasure.

Then, not knowing what else to do,
he wished her good day
and she continued on her aimless journey
with her dented shell in tow.

Ebba didn't get too far ahead until she noticed change.
Not only did her surroundings appear different,
they *felt* different.

She may have been discovering new creatures
or was simply viewing them with a new perspective.

She saw new colors.
She saw new parings.
She felt a desire.

Then it hit her...

Ebba had resiliently started life alone,
floating nowhere in particular,
but she didn't want to just float along anymore.
She wanted to *swim* and swim purposefully.
She needed to stay connected.

Life was lonely enough.
She was ready to share it with a friend,
and she knew just who she wanted that friend to be.

Ebba swam back to where she felt
most connected.
Where her heart felt light.
She swam back towards,
what she now realized was,
a loved one...

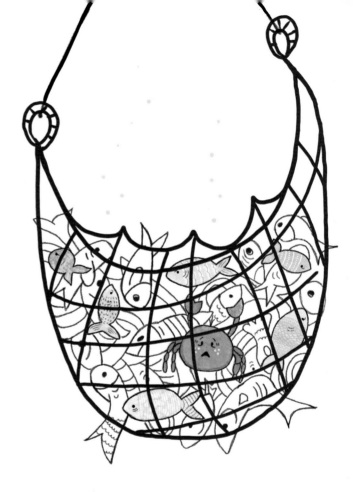

...IRVING!

Dear, sweet Irving was now in need of rescuing.
He had accidentally been scooped up by a fishing net
during one of his afternoon naps.

His warm demeanor was slipping away
until he saw Ebba's familiar face.

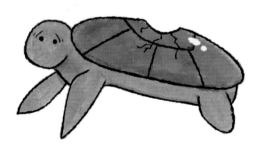

Her encouraging words and hopeful presence kicked in his wits.
He came up with a **SHARP** idea
that was sure to work.

He placed the ropes between his claws,

snapped them shut with all this might,

and...

. . . "You're free!"

The net broke open and Irving landed tenderly on Ebba's back,
fitting perfectly into the dent of her shell.
It was then that both Ebba and Irving realized
how important friendship was.

They were done heading nowhere in particular.
They wanted to swim purposefully.
They needed to be connected.

They now understood that love encourages you.
It supports you.
It fills in the cracks of lonely hearts...

...and even shells.

N ow this is...
Ebba *and* Irving.

Coming next!...

Parents, Teachers, & Therapists:

Questions for young readers to support insight and critical thinking

1.) WHY DO YOU THINK EBBA WAS THE ONLY ONE IN HER NEST?

2.) WHAT STRUGGLES DO YOU THINK EBBA ENDURED ON HER WAY TO THE OCEAN?

3.) WHAT DID EBBA NOTICE ABOUT THE STING RAYS, JELLY FISH, AND WHALES?

4.) WHY DO YOU THINK EBBA SANK DOWN INTO THE OCEAN FLOOR?

5.) WHERE DID THE ANCHOR COME FROM?

6.) HOW DID IRVING LIFT THE ANCHOR?

7.) HOW DID EBBA FEEL AFTER IRVING FREED HER FROM THE ANCHOR?

8.) WHAT CHANGES DID YOU NOTICE IN EBBA AFTER BEING FREED FROM THE ANCHOR?

9.) WHY DID EBBA SWIM BACK TO IRVING?

10.) WHY WAS IRVING ALWAYS NAPPING?

11.) WHY DID EBBA AND IRVING STICK TOGETHER IN THE END?

12.) WHAT WAS THE SCARIEST / HAPPIEST / SADDEST PART OF THE BOOK?

13.) WHO WOULD YOU WANT TO BE FRIENDS WITH?

14.) HAVE YOU EVER FELT LIKE YOU'VE HAD AN ANCHOR ON YOUR BACK? HOW DID YOU GET IT OFF?

Sarah A. Schroeder, LCSW

Mother, wife, sister, psychotherapist, and child development specialist, Sarah has been practicing child and family psychotherapist since 2010. Sarah finds inspiration from her loving family, resilient clients, brilliant educators and colleagues, and personal experiences. Originally from Los Angeles, California Sarah lives with her wonderful husband and two beautifully brilliant children in Evanston, Illinois.

Christopher Schroeder

Father, husband, brother, public health specialist, and scientific publisher, Chris takes his inspiration from his first hand experience providing health care and mental wellness advocacy in Uganda, Africa. Originally from Manhattan, New York Chris lives with his beloved and beautiful wife and two children in Evanston, Illinois.

PSALM 83:18